Mermaid Sister

Mary Ann Fraser

WALKER & COMPANY   NEW YORK

To Bryan

First published in the United States of America in 2008 by Walker Publishing Company, Inc.
Distributed to the trade by Macmillan

For information about permission to reproduce selections from this book, write to Permissions,
Walker & Company, 175 Fifth Avenue, New York, New York 10010 • www.walkeryoungreaders.com

Library of Congress Cataloging-in-Publication Data
Fraser, Mary Ann.
Mermaid sister / Mary Ann Fraser.
p.   cm.
Summary: Shelly has always wanted a sister, so when she meets Coral,
a mermaid, and brings her home, it seems like her wish has been granted.
ISBN-13: 978-0-8027-9746-9 • ISBN-10: 0-8027-9746-6 (hardcover)
ISBN-13: 978-0-8027-9747-6 • ISBN-10: 0-8027-9747-4 (reinforced)
[1. Mermaids—Fiction. 2. Sisters—Fiction. 3. Family life—Fiction.] I. Title.
PZ7.F86455Me 2008   [E]—dc22   2007037142

Book design by Alyssa Morris • Typeset in Hank & Billhead • The art was created with acrylic paint on paper
Printed in China
(hardcover) 10 9 8 7 6 5 4 3 2 1
(reinforced) 10 9 8 7 6 5 4 3 2 1

My brother, Gordy, is a pain in the patootie.

What I really want is a sister. I have a plan.

I throw the bottle into the ocean and wait.

In no time at all, my plan works. "My name is Shelly," I say. "Would you like to be my sister? Of course, that means Gordy would be your brother, too."

"My name is Coral," she says. "I've always wanted a sister, and Gordy can't be worse than my little brother, Sandy. Sandy is a pain in the flipper."

With the next big wave I take her to meet my family.

"This isn't like keeping a pet fish," says my father. "Would I have to make tuna casserole every night?" asks my mother.

"She smells," says my brother.

But when everyone sees how determined we are, they agree to give it a try.

I want Coral to feel welcome, so I let her watch
HER favorite shows.

I also make her peanut butter
and jellyfish sandwiches.

She especially likes to put salt
and seaweed in the tub and sing
whale songs.

Soon she is settled in—very settled in.

You can tell we are sisters because we are so much alike.
We both like to dance. I do hip-hop; she does flip-flop.

We both read the newspaper. I read the comics; she reads the tide charts.

And we both agree Gordy is a
pain in the patootie.

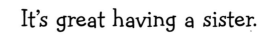

It's great having a sister.

I can do things with her I
can't do with a little brother.

But guess what. My mermaid sister can be a pain in the patootie, too. She leaves scales on my favorite blouse and keeps her tuna can collection in my closet.

AND she plays with Gordy.
That was not part of the plan.

We have our first sister fight.

It gets a little rough . . .

. . . and then a little quiet.

Then we make up.

I think something is still bothering Coral. I have a plan — a day at the beach to cheer her up.

My plan works, and we are all having a great time, until . . .

Coral wants to go home.

I know I'm going to miss my mermaid sister.
But guess what . . .

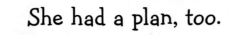

She had a plan, too.